This Little Tiger
book belongs to:

_____

_____

_____

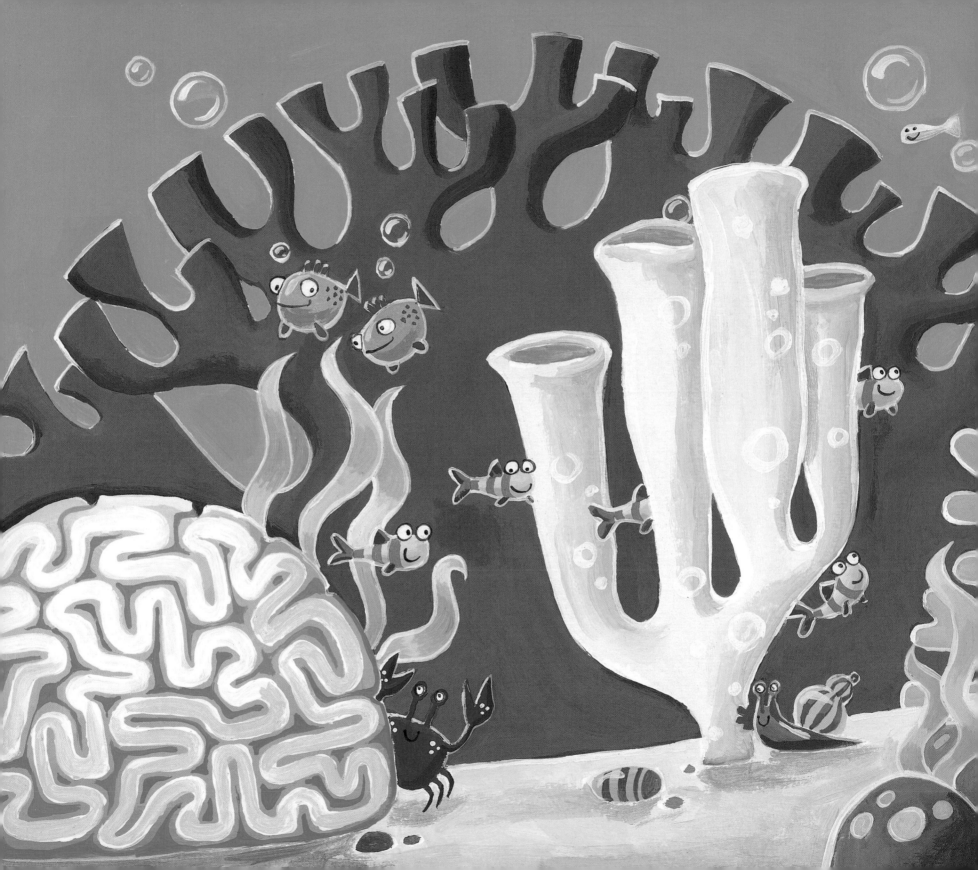

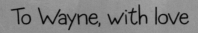

To Wayne, with love

LITTLE TIGER PRESS
An imprint of Magi Publications
1 The Coda Centre, 189 Munster Road,
London SW6 6AW
www.littletigerpress.com

First published in Great Britain 2003
This paperback edition published 2003

ISBN 1 85430 862 9

A CIP catalogue record for this book is available
from the British Library

Printed in Belgium by Proost

3 5 7 9 10 8 6 4

Smiley Shark

Ruth Galloway

Little Tiger Press
London

Far away, in a deep rolling ocean, lived Smiley Shark . . .
the smiliest and sunniest, the friendliest and funniest,
the biggest and toothiest of all the fish.

Every day Smiley Shark watched the beautiful fish
that dipped and dived and jiggled and jived,
and darted and dashed with a splosh and a splash.

Smiley Shark longed to dip and dive
with them. But whenever he smiled at the
other fish they swam away.

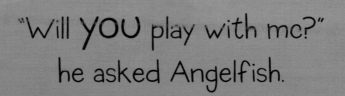

"Will **YOU** play with me?"
he asked Angelfish.

Angelfish shivered and shook,
then raced away as fast as she could swim.

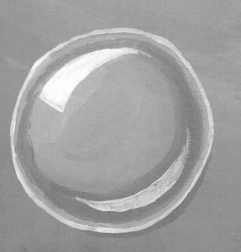

Pufferfish was blowing bubbles.
"That looks fun!" laughed Smiley Shark.
But Pufferfish blew himself up into
a big spiky ball and pricked poor
Smiley Shark on the nose!

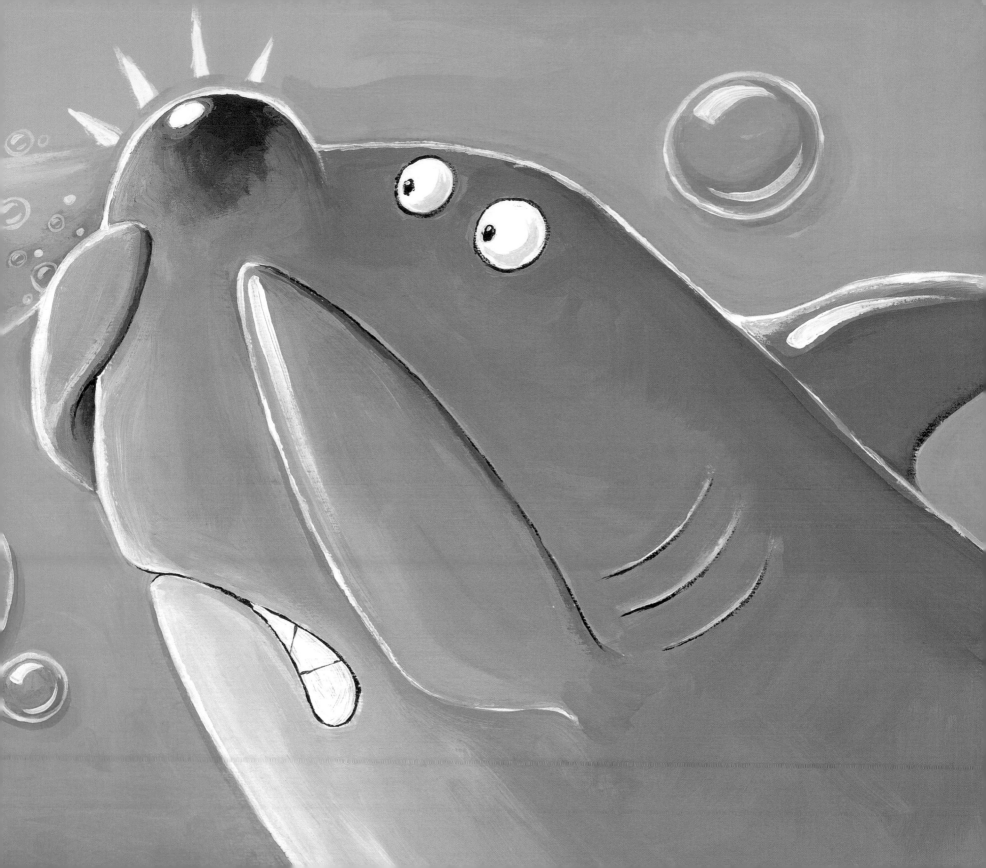

Starfish was twirling and whirling,
dancing and prancing.
"What fun!" giggled Smiley Shark.
But Starfish cartwheeled off across the
ocean floor as far away as she could go.

SWIRL!

Smiley Shark flashed his
grin at Jellyfish . . .

and Octopus . . .

and Catfish.

Off they swam,
as far from Smiley Shark
as they could get.

"Everyone is scared of my big white teeth,"
wailed Smiley Shark. He didn't feel much
like smiling any more.

SPLISH! SPLASH!

Twisting and turning, splashing and churning,
the fish danced faster than ever. Smiley Shark
watched from a distance. But this time something
was very wrong. All the fish were . . .

TRAPPED!

"Help!" cried the fish.
"Please help us, Smiley Shark!"

Smiley Shark swam round and
round the fisherman's net.
What could he do? How could he help?
The only thing Smiley Shark could do was . . .

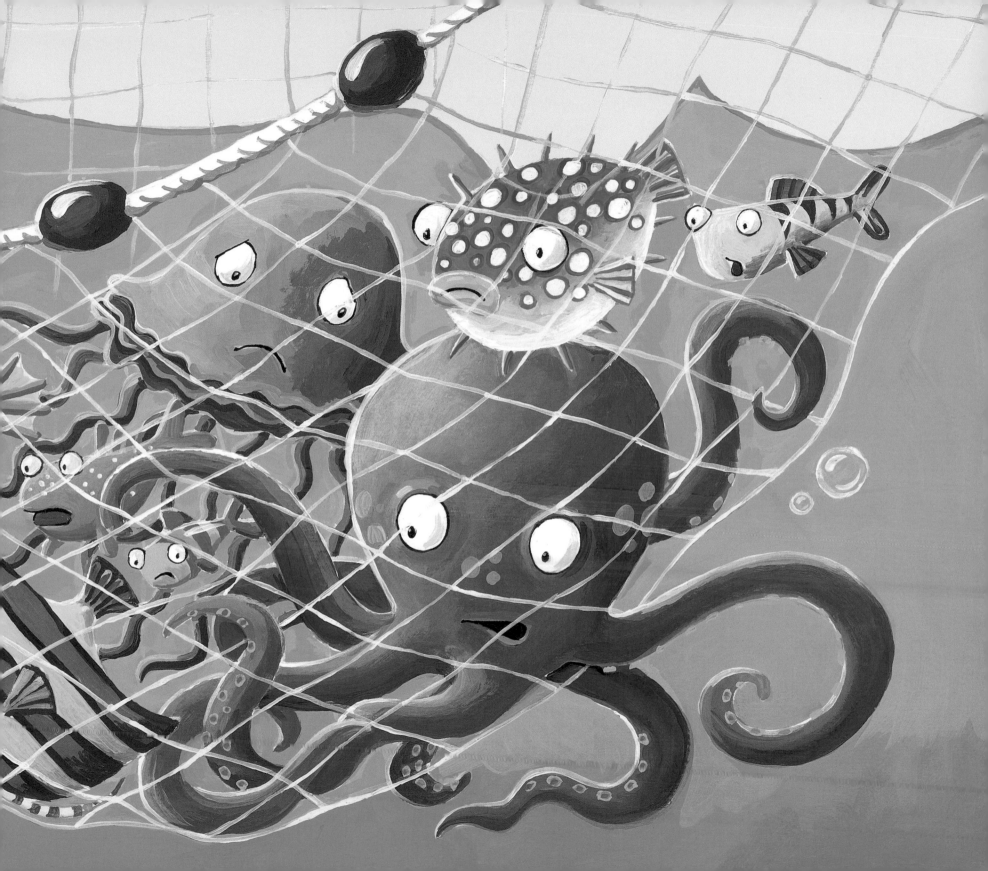

SMILE!

"AAAaaaaaaarghhh!" screamed the fisherman, dropping his heavy net into the waves. "I'm off!" he cried.

"Hurrah!" cheered the fish.
"We're safe! Thank you, Smiley Shark!"

Now far away, in the deep rolling ocean,
Smiley Shark and his friends can be seen,
dipping and diving, darting and dashing,
sploshing and splashing and

SMILING!

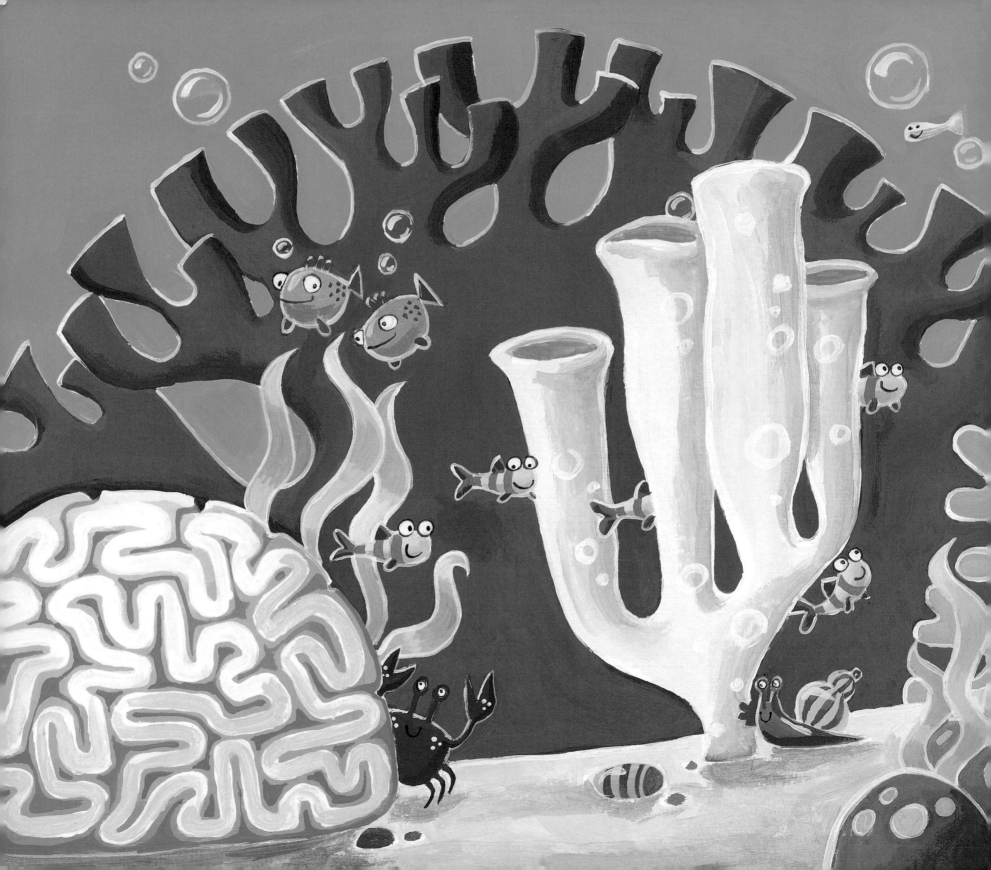

Dive into a book from Little Tiger Press

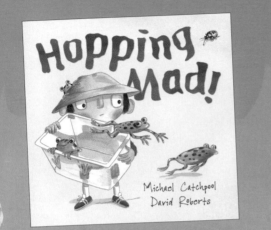

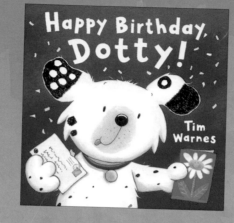

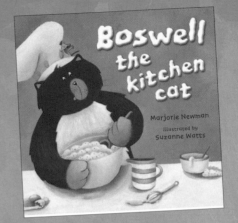

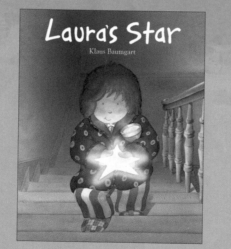

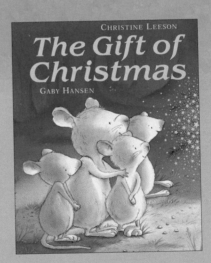

For information regarding any of the above
titles or for our catalogue, please contact us:
Little Tiger Press, 1 The Coda Centre,
189 Munster Road, London SW6 6AW, UK
Tel: 020 7385 6333 Fax: 020 7385 7333
e-mail: info@littletiger.co.uk www.littletigerpress.com